Ten Black Dots
Donald Crews

Greenwillow Books, *An Imprint of* HarperCollins *Publishers*

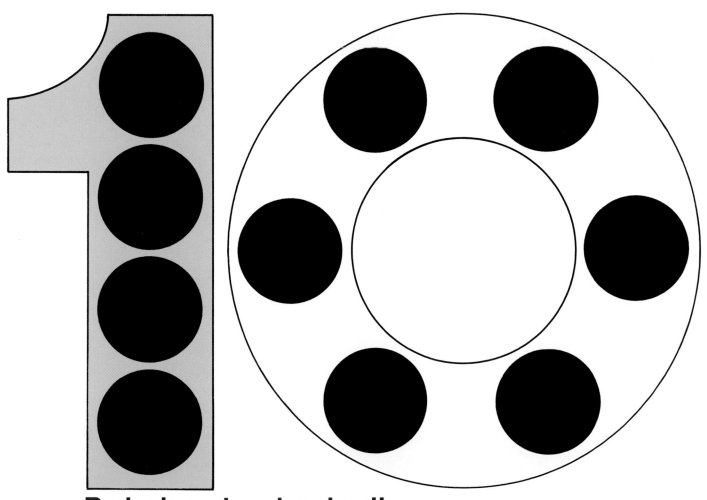

Redesigned and revised!

For Louis
whom I just
met, and
Nina & Amy
whom I've
known a
good while

The four-color preseparated
art was printed in red,
yellow, blue, and black.
The typeface is Helvetica Bold.

Ten Black Dots
Copyright © 1968, 1986
by Donald Crews
All rights reserved.
Manufactured in China.
For information address
HarperCollins Children's
Books, a division of
HarperCollins Publishers,
10 East 53rd Street,
New York, NY 10022.
www.harperchildrens.com
First Edition
12 13 SCP 30 29 28 27 26
25 24 23 22 21 20

Library of Congress
Cataloging-in-Publication Data
Crews, Donald.
Ten black dots.
Summary: A counting book
which shows what can be
done with ten black dots—
one can make a sun,
two a fox's eyes, or
eight the wheels of a train.
[1. Counting.
2. Stories in rhyme]
I. Title
II. Title: 10 black dots
PZ8.3.C867Te 1986
[E]   85-14871
ISBN 0-688-06067-6 (trade)
ISBN 0-688-06068-4 (lib. bdg.)
ISBN 0-688-13574-9 (pbk.)

What can you do with ten black dots?

1 One dot
can make
a sun

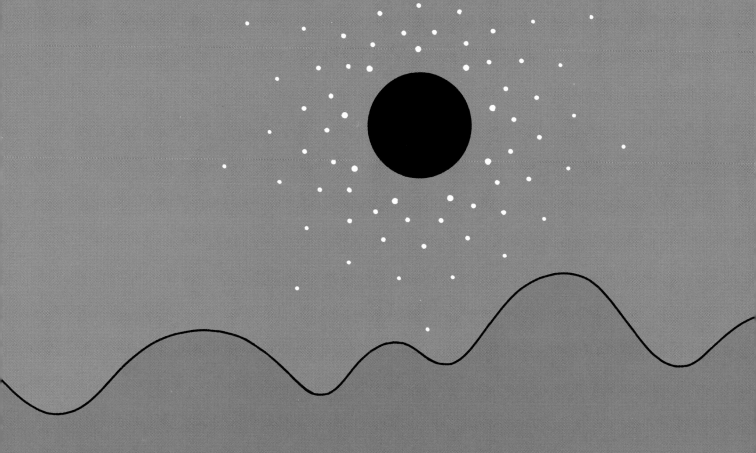

**or a moon
when day
is done.**

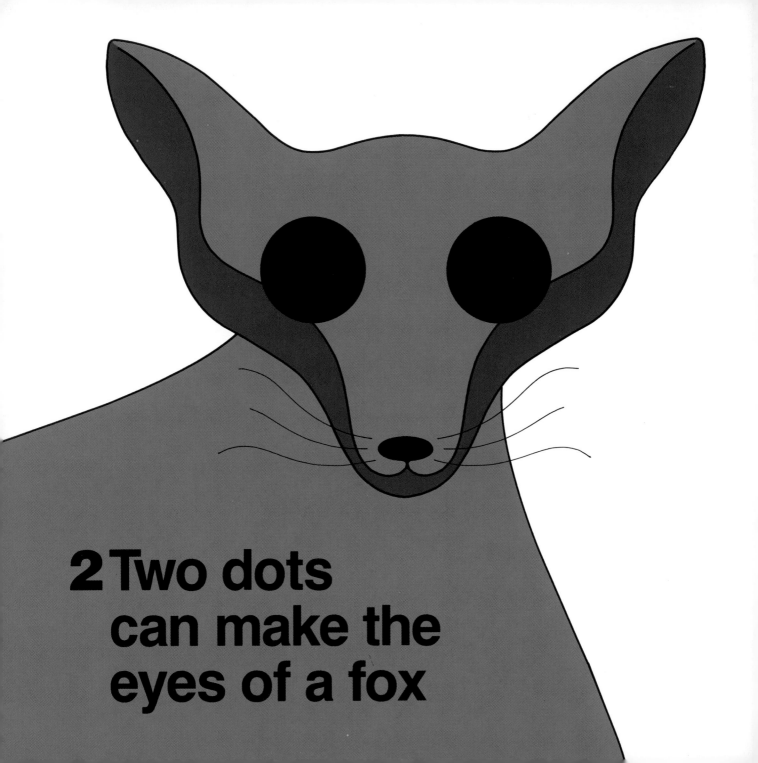

2 Two dots
can make the
eyes of a fox

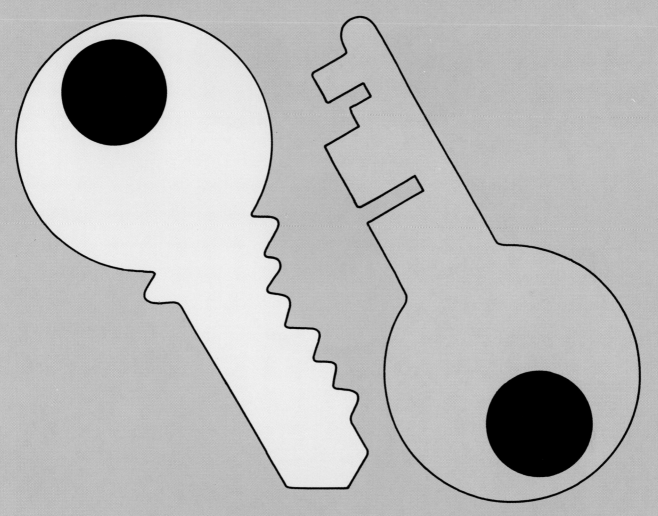

**or the eyes
of keys that
open locks.**

3 **Three dots
can make a
snowman's face**

**or beads
for stringing
on a lace.**

**4 Four dots
can make seeds from
which flowers grow**

**or the
knobs on
a radio.**

5 Five dots
can make buttons
on a coat

**or the
portholes
of a boat.**

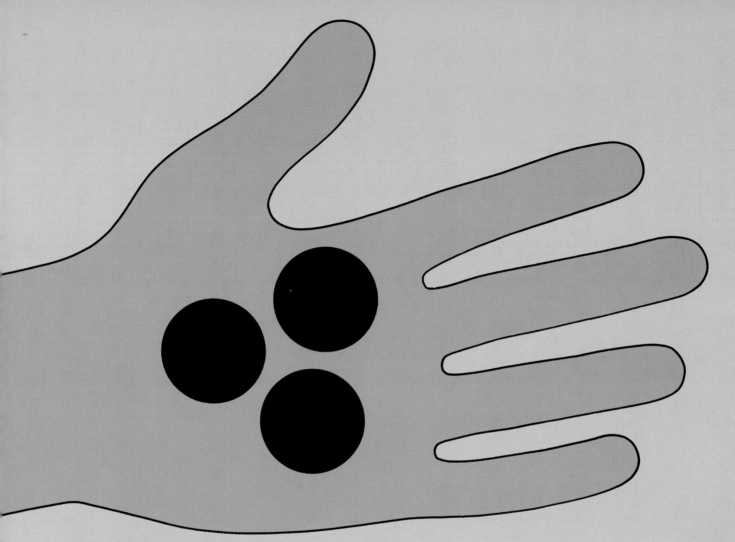

**6 Six dots
can make marbles
that you hold—**

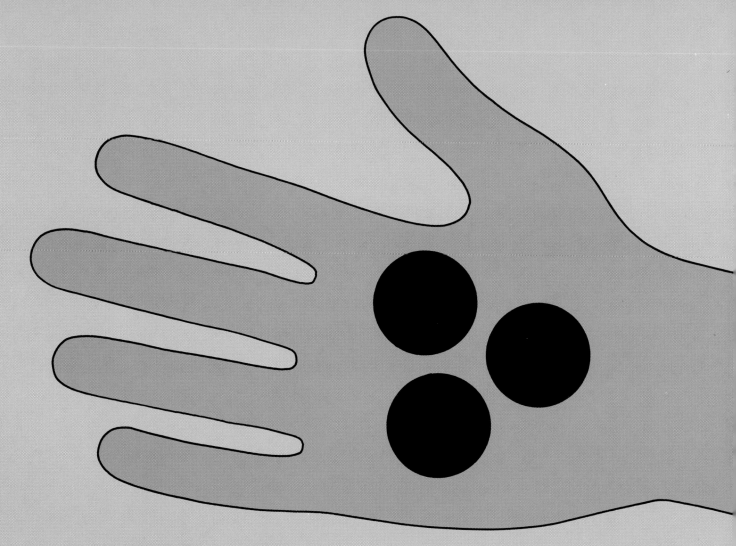

**half are
new, the rest
are old.**

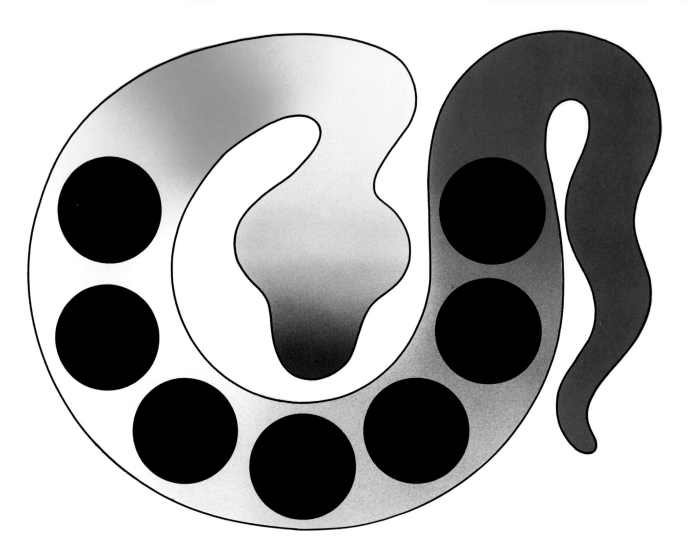

7 Seven dots
can make the spots
on a snake

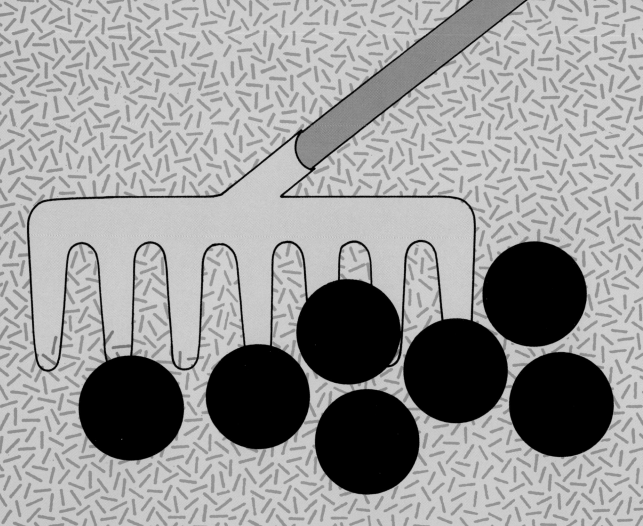

**or stones
turned up by a
garden rake.**

**8 Eight dots
can make the
wheels of a train**

**carrying freight
through sun
and rain.**

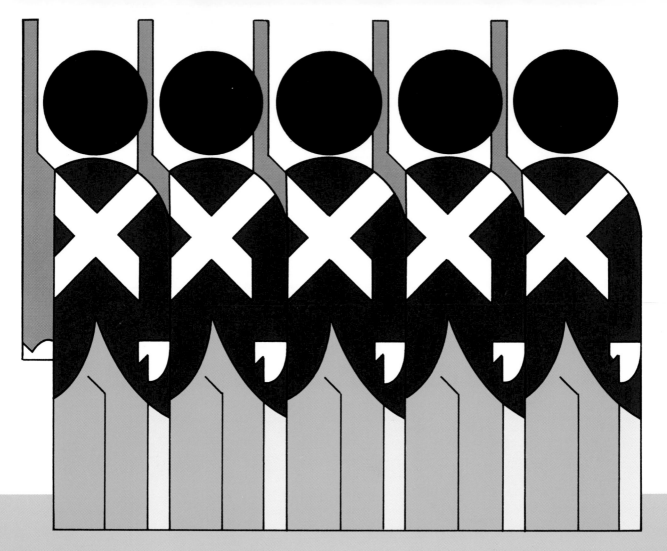

9 **Nine dots
can make toy soldiers
standing in rank**

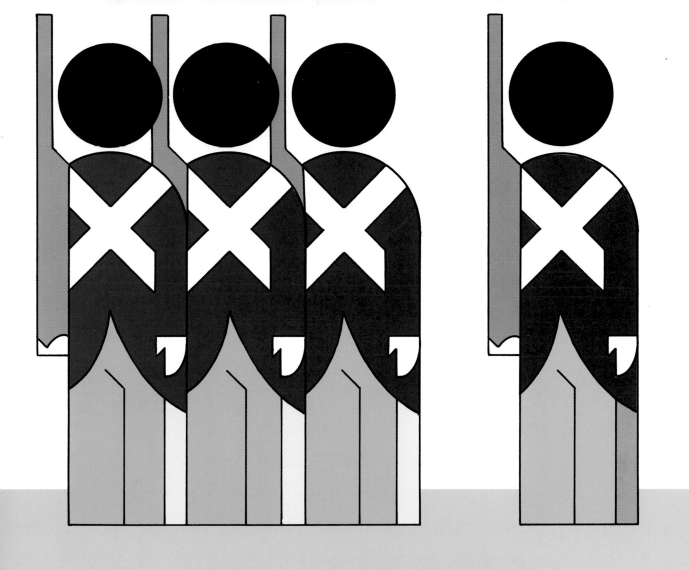

**or the pennies
in your
piggy bank.**

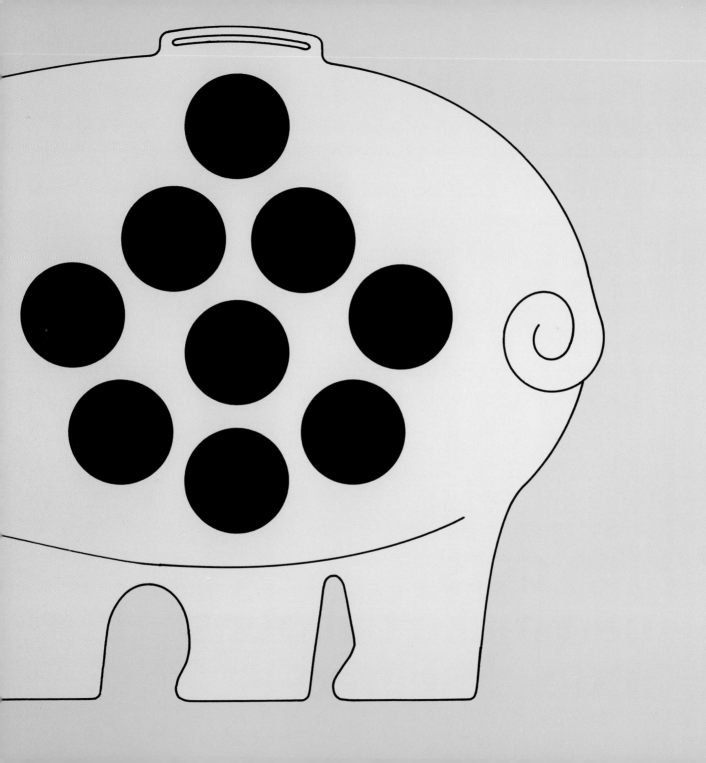

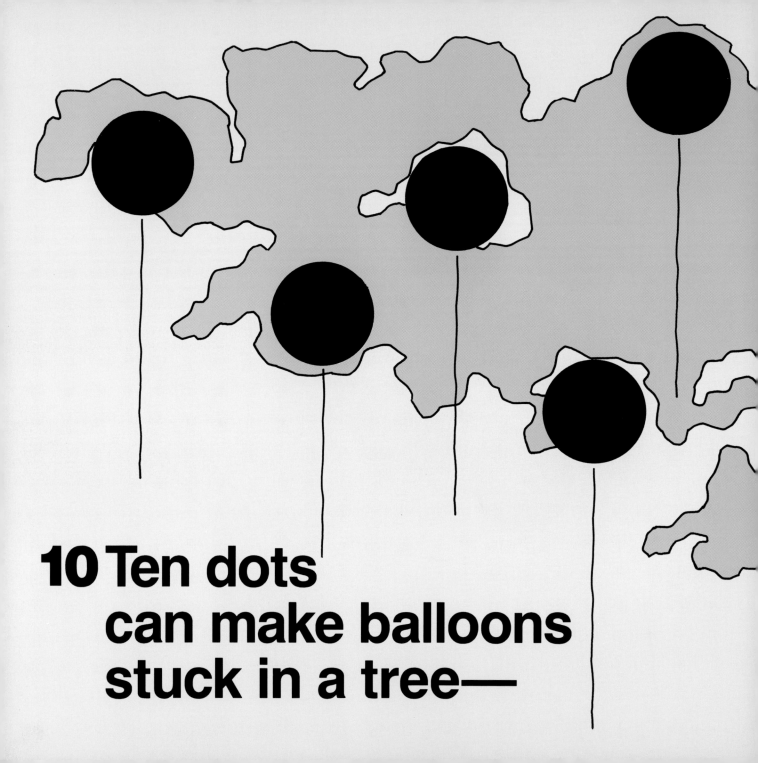

10 **Ten dots
can make balloons
stuck in a tree—**

**shake the branch
and set
them free.**

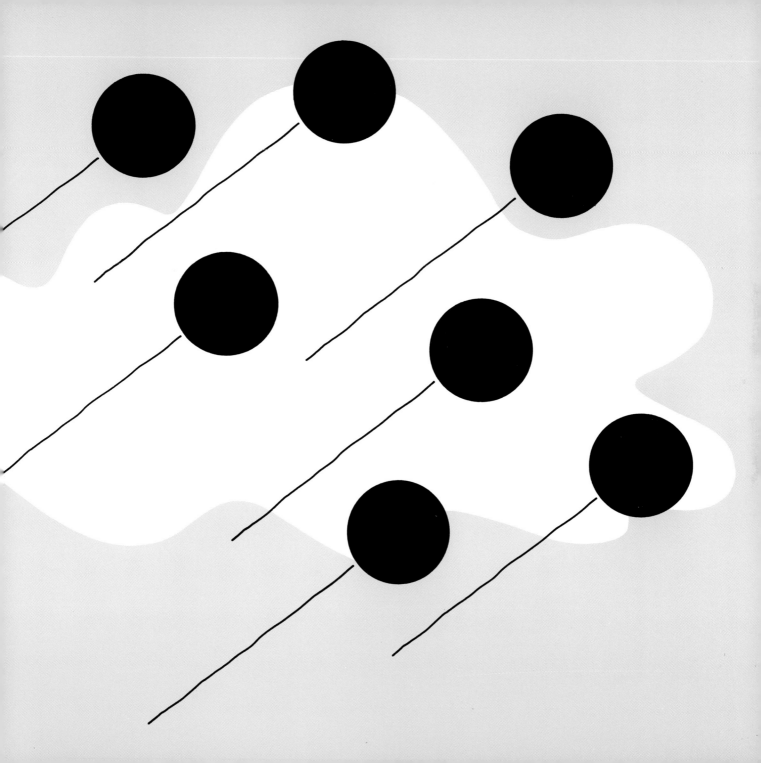

Count
them.
Are there
really ten?
Now we
can begin
again,
counting
dots
from one
to ten.

1

2

3

4

5

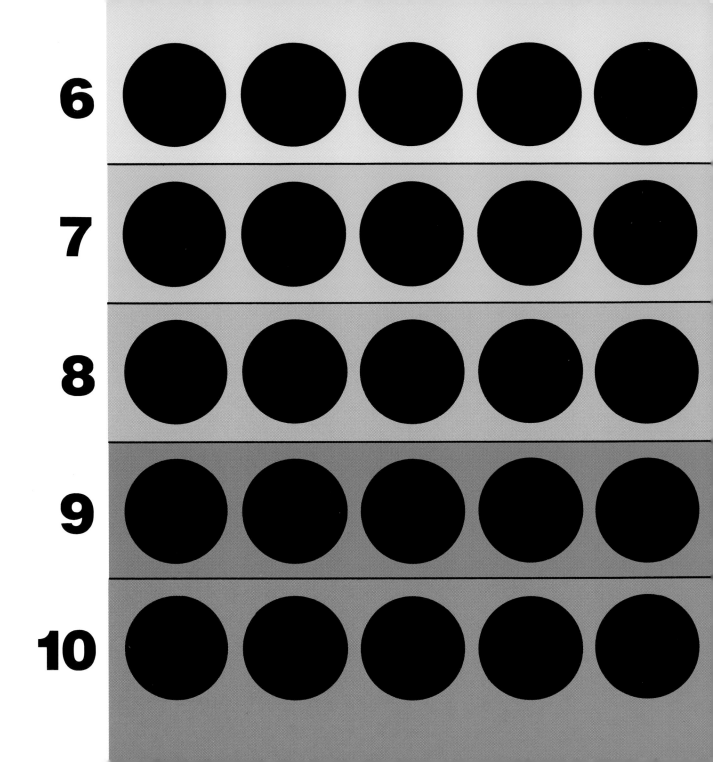